With This Ring

AMY LAURENS

OTHER WORKS

SANCTUARY SERIES

Where Shadows Rise
Through Roads Between
When Worlds Collide

KADITEOS SERIES

How Not To Acquire A Castle
Define Good
How Not To Ring The Hero's Bell (2020)

STORM FOXES SERIES

A Fox of Storms and Starlight

SHORTER WORKS

Darkness and Good
Dreaming Of Forests
Of Sea Foam and Blood
Trust Issues

NON-FICTION

How To Write Dogs
How To Theme
How To Create Cultures
How To Create Life
How To Map
The 32 Worst Mistakes People Make About Dogs

Find other works by the author at
www.amylaurens.com

With This Ring

INKLET #36

AMY LAURENS

Inkprint PRESS

www.inkprintpress.com

Print ISBN: 978-1-925825-35-0
eBook ISBN: 9781393027706

www.inkprintpress.com

National Library of Australia Cataloguing-in-Publication Data
Laurens, Amy 1985 –
With This Ring
52 p.
ISBN: 978-1-925825-35-0
Inkprint Press, Canberra, Australia
1. Fiction—Fantasy—Contemporary 2. Fiction—Fairy
Tales, Folk Tales, Legends & Mythology 3. Fiction—
Short Stories

First Print Edition: June 2020
Cover design © Inkprint Press
Interior art © Amy Laurens

WITH THIS RING

Orkney slipped into the cool water with barely a splash. The evening afterglow had faded from the horizon, and the river was quiet and still. He shivered in anticipation. Perhaps tonight Faroe would accept him.

A rustle from the riverbank drew his attention upwards. He found himself staring into a pair of stunning blue eyes, the kind one could drown in…

∞

Orkney shifted in the pre-dawn light and stretched into wakefulness. He blinked, disoriented by the room he found himself in. What was this place, with its smooth, even walls and the ceiling so high above his head? What was this softness he lay on, covered by layers and layers of warmth?

The room brightened and the first morning sunbeam shot over the horizon, straight through the clear pane in the wall and into his face. Orkney flinched, shying away from the heat on his fur.

His heart leapt. Not fur. Skin.

He glanced down and his eyes widened. How had he gotten into his human form? He didn't remember Changing.

Orkney concentrated, taking deep, even breaths. He remembered waking yesterday evening—at least he hoped it was yesterday. He'd stretched, scratched, crawled out of his burrow, and slipped into the stream. He'd meant to swim over to Faroe's, maybe ask what she was doing for a few hours. After all, it was June. She'd choose a mate any day now.

He remembered a noise, something distracting him. He'd looked up, right into a pair of beautiful, blue, human eyes.

Human.

The word tickled his consciousness, and he rolled over. Human.

He inhaled. Facing him, lashes curling on her sleep-softened cheeks, dark hair splaying on the pillow in waves and soft, tangled curls, lay the most exquisite woman.

The sun rose further and golden rays fell across her face, burnishing her skin and revealing copper high-lights in her hair.

Who was this beauty?

She opened her eyes.

Orkney gasped, shocked by their

intense blueness. The dream of burrows and fur fells away, and he remembered who she was.

A dimple sprang to life in Lia's cheek. "Morning, sexy."

He grinned. "Morning, gorgeous." He reached out and drew her into his arms. The warmth reminded him of something—a burrow, perhaps?—but Lia pressed up against him and he could feel every curve and hollow, and nothing else mattered for the next few minutes.

By the time they'd finished he had decided that he must have dreamed of water and fur, and as they broke apart he sighed. "Lia?"

"Mm?" She lay with her eyes closed again, breasts rising and falling with her breaths.

"I love you."

Her lashes parted. For a moment she stared up at him, then her lips curved into a soft smile. "I love you, too."

Lia had left not long after breakfast on some errand or other, and Orkney found himself wandering through the house. Though he'd seen it all before, today it felt new and unique, and he was enjoying poking into all the odd corners and crannies.

Even if his gaze did keep drifting to the strange brownish-yellow ring on the third finger of his left hand.

Given Lia's happiness and the twin ring on her third left finger, he guessed he must have given in at long last and proposed. He felt slightly squirmy at the fact that he couldn't remember it, but Lia hadn't said anything, so perhaps he wouldn't be expected to discuss it.

He tiptoed out of the spare room, closing the door behind him. One room to go: Lia's study. He grasped the handle and his pulse began to race.

He frowned. He'd been in here plenty of times before.

Shaking it off, he turned the knob and pushed open the door. For a long moment he paused in the doorway. The air inside was still and uninviting. No dust danced in the sunlight, and the books that lined the walls seemed to hold their breaths.

Orkney realised he'd been holding his, and exhaled. Books couldn't hold their breaths. Nonsense.

He strode towards the nearest wall, bending over to stare the books in the spine.

"Myths of Northern Scotland," he read aloud. He blinked as a memory hit him. Lia had always loved northern Scottish folklore. Icelandic, too. She loved everything from that part of the world and longed to visit. It was an expensive trip from Australia—but maybe he'd try to save up and take her for their honeymoon.

He pulled the book from the shelf and crossed the room to Lia's desk. Seating himself behind the desk, he opened the book at random. "As soon as the seal was clear of the water its skin sloughed away to reveal a man, dark-haired like the seal and strong." He flicked a few pages. "...woman went to the sea and wept seven tears. Right away the seal came to her..."

Orkney tilted his head, wondering why the book sounded so familiar. He'd never read it before—he'd never read *any* of Lia's books before, he made a point of it—so how could he know these words?

A glimmer of light caught the corner of his eye, and he glanced sideways and down. He exhaled, muscles relaxing—just a drawer handle, catching the morning light. Nothing to worry about.

But something about it held his attention, and he peered closer.

"Huh." His nostrils twitched as he realised it was made of the same stone as the ring that encircled his finger. He opened the drawer.

His eyes widened. It was empty but for a single ornate key, larger than his hand. The shaft and handle of the key were wrought in the same stone, animal figures leaping and twining their way along it.

I wonder what it opens, he thought, turning it over in his hands. Like the words in the book, he knew he'd never seen it before—but it seemed familiar. Like it was connected to him.

He sat back, staring aimlessly around the room. He frowned as his gaze came to rest on the large windows, covered by thick drapes. Either the windows were a lot wider than they looked, or the curtains were covering a large portion of wall. How odd.

Key in hand, Orkney tiptoed over

and pulled back the curtain. He gasped. A large wooden door greeted him, bound with strips of iron and secured with a heavy stone padlock.

He glanced down at the key. Couldn't hurt to try...

The key slid into the lock and turned with a well-oiled click. Orkney pulled off the padlock and cracked open the door.

A musty smell met his nose, damp and animal. He shivered and flicked on the light.

His mouth dried.

Shelves lined the walls, shelves covered—he bit back the bile—in bits and pieces of *animals*. Horse hooves, several sets of different-sized antlers, a fox's bushy tail—even the damp, rubbery skins of some frogs. A thick, grey seal pelt took up one of the back shelves, and above it...

Orkney gasped. Treading carefully, he moved towards the strange object.

It looked almost like a duck's bill, except it was brownish-grey and much broader. He knew what it was, of course—he saw it almost every day, on the back of his twenty-cent coins—but his mind didn't want to bend around what it meant.

He drew a deep breath. Inching his fingers closer, he strained his ears for any sign that Lia might have returned. If she found him here, with this…

A shiver ran down his spine. She couldn't.

His fingertip brushed the platypus bill and he froze, knowing that if any moment was the one for Lia to burst in, this was it.

But she didn't. He snatched up the bill and raced out into the study, slamming the secret door behind him.

The river. He had to get to the river.

Orkney crouched on the riverbank, leaning against a gum tree and peering into the shallows. He had to move quickly, but he couldn't rush the little creatures—and he had to see them, just to make sure.

Adrenalin surged through his chest as the water rippled and a sleek, brown body resolved from the murky shadows. The platypus confirmed his fears—but it also tugged at his consciousness, and Orkney felt that somehow it ought to be familiar to him.

He waited as it broke the surface and hovered in place, taking a breath.

"Come on," he muttered. "Turn around."

As if in response, the platypus turned. Orkney gasped. *Faroe*. The platypus's name was Faroe.

Orkney backed up a few steps so as not to disturb her, then glanced down at the bill clasped in his fingers. There could be no doubt, now. He steeled himself, took the bill in his fingertips and pressed it to his face.

Nothing happened. His stomach fell.

He pressed it harder against his nose and thought 'platypus' with all his might.

"It's not going to work."

He jumped and whipped the bill into his pocket. *Oh no.* "You're not going to take it from me!"

Lia shrugged. "It doesn't matter. It won't work now."

Orkney's jaw twitched. "Why not?"

Lia raised an eyebrow. "You can't guess?"

Orkeny's gaze flicked down to the ring, then back to Lia.

She confirmed his guess with a sly smile. "Indeed."

"Get back!" Orkney stepped back and hunched down to the ground.

She laughed. "Or what? You're a platykie. A small part of you may be human, but most of you, my sexy little beast, is platypus. They're not known for their aggression." She paced toward him, eyes trained on his.

Orkney's blood began to race, pounding past his ears and pulsing in his neck. He tried to look bold. "So what?" he said. "I can't change with the ring on. I can always take it off."

Lia showed her teeth in a crocodile-grin. "Go on, then. Try it."

Orkney's stomach knotted, but he took a firm grip and tugged on the ring. His eyebrows shot up as it slipped easily along his finger, and relief spread through his body.

Lia's grin didn't waver, and Orkney felt a tiny prod of doubt.

But the ring was still slipping freely, coming right—

He frowned and tugged harder.

Lia's grin broadened.

He looked down at the ring and tugged again. It wasn't even *touching* his finger, but it refused to slide off the end.

Lia resumed her stalk towards him. "Platykies." She snorted. "You're the easiest Changelings in the world to trap." She tilted her head as Orkney sank to the ground. "Even the seals put up *some* sort of fight."

Orkney wasn't listening. A strange prickling had come over his knees and he frowned, trying to figure out why.

Lia shrugged. "Well, I guess I'm not going to complain."

Faroe.

An image burst into Orkney's mind of Faroe, swimming in a rare beam of light, tail pulsing as she propelled herself down towards the river bed.

He recalled the hunger he'd had for her, the instinct that had welled, reminding him the venomous spurs on his hind legs weren't just for show.

He would fight for her, when the time came.

Lia looked down at him, hands on hips, and laughed. "You're too easy, you know that?"

The time had come. Orkney leapt to his feet and thrust his knee at Lia, pivoting to lend it extra force.

Lia screeched and toppled backwards, head aimed straight at an outcrop of sharp granite rocks. The terror on her face turned Orkney's stomach to lead. He didn't want to *kill* her.

He leapt forward and grasped her left hand. He thought he had her, but her weight jolted up his arm and his fingers slipped.

Lia screamed as Orkney's nails raked her hand and fingers. She thudded to the ground, head narrowly missing the rocks. She glared up at Orkney. "You!"

Orkney recoiled from the venom in her voice.

"Give. That. Back." She shoved herself to her feet.

Orkney's brow creased. "What?" A pressure against his palm caught his attention and he opened his fist. He blinked. A ring, the smaller twin of his, lay in his cupped hand. "Oh."

Lia limped forward, scowling. "Just give it here, Orkney, and everything will be fine."

He stared at the ring. Why was it tingling? He sucked in a breath as his own ring began to tingle in response. He glanced at Lia.

She lunged.

He ducked aside, grabbing at his own ring and tearing it off. As Lia straightened Orkney threw the rings out into the river.

Lia screamed her rage and lunged again.

Orkney whipped out the platypus bill and pressed it to his face. He ducked Lia's outstretched arms and closed his eyes, focussing with all his might on Changing.

Shivers crawled over his skin as the world grew large around him.

Lia shrieked and threw herself to the ground after him, wrapping her fingers around his broad tail. He wriggled and tried to flick free of her hands, but she pinned him tight. "Stay *still!*" she hissed. "I'll have a Platykie for my collection even if I have to kill you to do it!"

He drew a hind leg forward and fell still.

Lia chuckled.

As her grip beginning to slacken, Orkney kicked his leg backwards. His spur found her hand and buried itself deep into her skin. She screamed and flung her hands into the air, and Orkney found himself tumbling toward the river.

Lia scrabbled after him, sobbing and fumbling. He found the lip of the bank and leaped into the water, grabbing a quick lungful of air before diving.

The wave Lia caused as she jumped in after him tossed him around like a twig.

He turned his head, waving his nose back and forth to reorient himself, drawing a mental picture from the electrical and mechanical impulses that reached him.

Lia's hair floated out from her face, clouding like weed, and she flailed her arms as she fought her natural buoyancy and dove after him.

Orkney paddled for his life, reaching the bottom and ducking under a branch.

Still Lia followed, tearing the branch away and snatching at his tail.

He shot forward towards an overhang. *Please, let there be shelter!*

Relief washed over him as he drew closer and detected a hole in the bank. He swam in, tucked his tail, and turned around, ready to back away if Lia came close.

He waited for a moment. Nothing.

Pulse racing, he crept towards the entrance and poked his bill out. He trembled at the wild impulses, terrified that he'd been tricked, that she'd been waiting for him to appear again so she could catch him.

But his brain caught up with the signals and he realised that the movements he was detecting were random, chaotic…

The movements had stopped five minutes ago, but Orkney still wasn't sure. His head was beginning to ache and he desperately needed some oxygen. His blood pounded past his ears and he felt his thoughts growing floaty. He had to go.

But what if she was lying in wait, and not dead at all?

He fluttered his tail, trying to decide.

A spasm passed through his lungs, and he knew it was move or die. He pushed out from the hole and streaked towards the surface.

Fresh air hit his nose and he gasped. His chest burned and he sucked the air in greedily, waiting for the pain to subside.

After a moment he turned, curious now about Lia. He couldn't see anything on the surface, so he ducked under and wagged his nose.

He shuddered.

Her body was there alright, entwined in the branches she'd snatched away.

He waggled again, feeling the electrical impulses from her body fade and die.

Water splashed behind him and he jumped to the surface.

"What's going on?"

His eyes widened as Faroe swam up and nudged his side.

"Nothing," he said.

"I don't think so. I felt the commotion from all the way around the bend." She nosed him up and down. "Are you okay?"

Orkney let his glance flick towards the submerged body, then back to Faroe. "I'm fine, now."

There was a *schplop* from behind him and Orkney's heart jolted.

Faroe froze, staring. "What... what is it?"

Orkney turned her around with his bill. "It's nothing, you don't need to see."

"Orkney, no, let me go." She twisted underneath the water and re-surfaced behind him.

He groaned.

"Orkney."

He turned and paddled up beside her.

"Orkney, it's a body."

"I know."

Faroe gave him a considering look. "What did you do?"

"Nothing, I swear!" His tail quivered and he lowered his voice. "It—she—tried to capture me. She put a ring on me, Faroe."

Faroe gasped. "No!"

"Yes."

Faroe nestled into his shoulder. "I'm sorry."

"It's okay," he said, rubbing his bill down her back. "I'm fine."

She shook him off. "Well." An impish light flickered in her eyes. "How about we make certain?"

"What do you mean?"

Faroe paddled around and offered him her tail. "Let's make sure it can't happen again."

Orkney hesitated. "Really?"

Faroe flicked her tail impatiently. "Really."

Orkney shivered in delight and surged forward, holding the base of her tail in his bill. He sighed as she paddled forward, towing him off towards her burrow.

The flicker out of the corner of his eye was just the sun on the water, he told himself. Not a ring. Just the sun.

THE MAKING OF
WITH THIS RING

I've always been fascinated with shapeshifters. I'm not quite sure why—and maybe I never will be. It's something about the human-animal connection—I'm attracted to stories where humans can commune with animals too, and shapeshifting hits the same squishies for me, but still, I can't quite articulate why.

This was the first shapeshifter story I ever wrote. I can't quite remember why, but it emerged out of the confluence of selkie mythology with the Australian biome.

We don't have large aquatic mammals—in fact, we don't have very many large mammals at all—but we do have platypuses. Platypuses plus selkie mythology? Yes please and thank you!

Maybe one day I'll take advantage of this little piece of mythology I've created and write another platykie story, but for now, this conveys the scope of what I wanted to explore: the feeling of being out of your own skin, trapped, and unable to recall your identity—and the lengths you might be willing to go to in order to regain your life.

P.S. Did you know that selkie mythology is tied firstly to the Faroe Islands, a Danish territory midway between Iceland and Norway in the cold North Atlantic Ocean, and also to Orkney, an archipelago off the north-east coast of Scotland? ☺

DOWNLOAD YOUR FREE EBOOK

When you buy a print book from Inkprint Press, we like to say THANK YOU by offering you the ebook for free!

Please head to www.inkprintpress.com/inklets/36/ and the use the coupon 36INK to get your copy of this Inklet in epub AND mobi today!
(Coupon will only work once.)

Read more by Amy Laurens!

A FOX OF STORMS AND STARLIGHT

CHAPTER ONE

SIX YEARS AGO, I SAVED A FOX IN THE bush. It was only because my dog died. At the time, it felt like a pretty crappy bargain.

It was the first day of autumn—not by the calendar, but by the fresh bite in the morning air, the golden quality of the light as it lit the main road through town in the mid afternoon.

Sailor was a big, black shaggy thing, something like a Newfoundland, a lively shadow in the golden light, and I was eleven.

I'm sorry to be starting any story this way, but the fact of the matter is, this where it all began.

I'll spare you the awful details. Enough to say that Sailor had got out of the yard somehow, and had been hit by a truck careening down the highway that split our tiny town in two as it blatantly ignored the speed limit.

I saw it happen.

And although I cradled him in my lap as the smell of burnt-out brakes and hot asphalt and turning leaves filled my nose, his giant, furry black head all of him I could fit, there was nothing I could do.

There was nothing anyone could do.

I knew that, but it didn't stop the knot of frustration and guilt in my chest, or the taste of bile in the back of my throat every time I closed my eyes and saw the truck hitting him, again and again and again.

It took years for that vision to fade.

But that evening, only a few hours after it had happened, everything still felt fresh, and raw.

Sunny, my sister, was only nine at the time. She cried for hours, just sobbing like she'd never breathe right again.

I'd cried a little, at the scene with Sailor's head lying in my lap as his big, brown eye stared up at nothing.

It had been mercifully fast, there was that.

And the driver had copped a massive fine—speeding, reckless driving, I think they even defected his truck—and came to visit us later, a big, pot-bellied man standing on our front verandah, shuffling his royal blue cap round and round and round in his hands as he apologised.

But that evening, with Sunny sobbing her heart out on the couch in the living room and Mum and Dad trying desperately to console her as dinner burned on the stove, I couldn't cry, even though the acrid scent of burning soy sauce, scorching brown sugar and smoking rice wine from the marinade prickled the back of my throat and the corners of my eyes.

I was the eldest, and I had to be responsible.

Possibly, if I'd been just a little more responsible, Sailor wouldn't have died.

So I slipped out the glass slider from the family room to the deck while Sunny cried, glancing up at the two storeys of our moody grey house behind me before jumping heavily down the three steps from the rail-less deck to the lawn, and set out for the gate in the back fence.

I couldn't cry, and I didn't want to add anything to an already chaotic and stressful situation inside—but I couldn't stay there, either.

In the gaps between the gum trees to the west, the sky tinged to red and gold at the horizon, the sun sinking slowly into oblivion. I'm pretty sure I didn't know the word oblivion back then, but I knew what it meant, how it felt—and I craved it, desperately.

Anything would be better than the gaping hole in my chest.

And so, because I didn't know where to find it or how to get there, I stalked through the bush, pushing myself until I breathed hard and my lungs ached and sweat ringed me, chasing the way that hard exercise elevated me over my constantly looping thoughts.

Directly above, dark, heavy clouds obscured the sky, and the air was thick, heavy, humid.

Beneath the smell of dry gum leaves and even drier dirt, I could catch a hint of ozone, and occasionally the wind turned cool for a breath as it gusted against my skin, promising a late evening storm.

I walked harder, faster, outrunning the video looping in my mind of the truck's impact.

When the first drops of rain spat at me from out of the sky, I barely noticed. My skin was filmed with sweat, slick and salty, and the peppering of rainwater barely added to it.

That was at first.

But within minutes, it became clear that those first pattering spits had been the early foreshadowing of a storm darker and more intense than any I remembered.

Thunder rolled across the sky, distant and grumbling at first, a lazy background chorus to the rhythmic melody of the rain as it splattered down on grey-green leaves and red-tinged twigs, turning the silvered bark of an old, dead gum to deep grey and making the spiky, tussocky grass seem oddly luminescent in the dying light.

I stood under a grey gum with stains down its trunk that the rain was turning orange, arms wrapped around myself, shivering hard—and for the briefest instant, thought about not going home.

Mum and Dad would pitch a fit.

And I had to be responsible.

I turned, dark t-shirt plastered to my skin, dark hair sticking to my face and clinging to my neck, and began trudging my way back. The storm closed over properly, clouds rolling over the horizon and cutting off the thin scythe of blood-coloured sky, making the bush dark and unwelcoming in the premature night.

Lightning flashed.

Thunder cracked hot on its heels.

I jumped—and stared hard at the gap between two ghost-barked trees, where for a second, I was sure I'd seen a pair of eyes.

Nothing moved.

Nothing except the drenching rain, anyway, weighing down the branches that tossed fitfully in the wind.

The smell of wet dirt and soaked bark rose around me, undercut by eucalypt and ozone.

If anything had the power to wash away the hurt inside me, this storm was it. I tipped my face to the sky, imagining the rain washing over me had the ability to wash me inside as well, and the raindrops splattered hard on my face.

More lightning. More thunder, cracking over top of the constant hiss of the falling rain.

And in the distance, something eerie, lifting the hairs on the back of my neck: a strange kind of high-pitched howl, a cry that rang with moonlight and distance, cutting straight through the noise of the storm.

Bolts of lightning streaked across the sky—one—two—three in the space of half a second, followed immediately by a growling crack of thunder so immense it vibrated in my chest. I ducked instinctively.

There, in the corner of my eye...

I froze, crouched with my arms over my head.

The strange cries came again—and they were closer.

I stared hard at the place, low to the ground, where I was sure I'd seen something small, maybe the size of a cat.

Flash. Growl.

Rain spitting down.

There. Right there. A small animal, pointy ears, light coloured chin and throat…

The strange, eerie cries came a third time, and my heart pounded fiercely. Whatever was making the noise, it was close. Really close.

The little creature across from me reacted too, flattening itself to the ground.

My jaw twitched.

My heart pounded.

My fingertips bit into my upper arms.

Stay? Go?

Run? Freeze?

The hairs on my neck prickled again and goosebumps broke out all over me.

Cold dread formed a knot in my stomach.

Something was coming.

Something worse than the storm.

I had to get home.

I made it halfway to standing—and a series of strange, awful noises made me freeze again. They were sharp, clacking, squealing sounds, like someone knocking two echoing stones against each other, interspersed with high-pitched yowling…

And the creature in the darkness screamed.

I threw my back against the gumtree behind me, pressing hard against it. My heart hammered.

I peered back and forth in the dark, eyes wide.

Rain drenched down, but my throat was dry.

My pulse pounded faster.

The little creature screamed again—and as lightning flashed, I saw it on its back, legs slashing wildly at the air as something attacked.

The awful, clicking-yowling noises grew louder.

I slapped my hands over my ears, gasping. Water ran down my face, getting into my mouth, my eyes.

It was hurting.

Whatever the small thing was, it was getting hurt, and I'd seen enough animals hurting today.

Something in my chest snapped.

I flung myself across the ground, leaping a couple of tussocks and a fallen branch before I crashed to my knees.

I crawled closer, desperate, gasping for air through the heavy curtains of rain.

I couldn't see it. Where?

Somewhere here, near the base of that tree…

The yowling screeched right next to my ear. I cowered against the ground, spiky grass pricking my face, wet-earth smell smothering me—but now, there was a strange mustiness too, a cousin to wet-dog smell.

At the next flash of lightning, I saw it.

The creature was a fox—and something barely visible was attacking it, only the gleam of eye or flicker of teeth visible in the gloom.

But the damage was real enough.

The little fox's side had been opened right up, and in the bright, stark flashes of heavenly electricity, the blood was dark, thinned by the constant rain.

No.

No more animals were going to die today.

Not when this time, I could do something about it.

I snatched at a branch on the ground that turned out to be more of a twig, and launched myself toward the creature.

I had no idea what was attacking it, but I screamed and waved my handful of twiggy leaves anyway, batting them in the air over the fox like I knew what I was doing.

The horrible clacking cries ceased.

With one long, low rumble, the rain began to ebb.

Still gasping for air, pulse galloping in my throat, I sat next to the fox and shifted it carefully into my lap, realising as I tasted salt that I was crying.

I huddled over, trying to shelter the poor creature from the slackening rain, running my fingers over its wiry cheek— over and over and over and over.

"Please," I sobbed, throat tight and aching, chest constricted. "Please. Please don't die. Please."

Another gust of cool air washed over the clearing, taking the last of the rain with it—and lifting the goosebumps on my arms again.

I shivered, drawing the fox close, like it was a stuffed animal I could hug for comfort—its or mine, I couldn't say.

"Please. Please don't die. Please."

Something shifted in my lap.

Around us, the world stilled, dazed from the storm, but also something more, something watching, something waiting, as the bush held its collective breath.

The only sound was the occasional drip of rainwater from the gum leaves onto a fallen log—no insects, no wind, no rustling of leaves. Just… stillness.

And the fox, who shivered in my lap.

The clouds tore open, revealing a ragged triangle of stars that glittered in the fox's eye as it blinked open and stared up at me.

My chest snagged.

My throat ached from crying, and a headache was forming in the back of my head. But the fox blinked up at me—alive.

I ran a finger down it again, from nose to cheek to ear to shoulder, all the way down its side to its thick, bushy tail—and the wound in its side began to close.

Laboriously, it hauled itself to its front legs.

I tried to stop it—"No, it's okay, you can stay here, I'll look after you"—but it lifted its top lip to show half-hearted teeth, and staggered away.

As it did, I thought perhaps its fur began to shrink. And suddenly, it looked larger in the night—as large as a dog, as large as Sailor…

But I blinked, and it was just a trick of the light, because the creature that darted away into the bushes like nothing was wrong at all was clearly a fox, the size of a large cat or maybe a small beagle, and nothing more.

And if something screamed in the night not long afterward, and the cry sounded horribly, horribly human?

Well. I was halfway back toward home again by then, and I pressed my fingertips to my lower eyelids and prayed my parents wouldn't murder me for getting home so late.

Keep reading! Head to www.amylaurens.com/ books/storm-foxes/ to buy your copy now!

ABOUT THE AUTHOR

AMY LAURENS is an award-winning Australian author of fantasy fiction for all ages. She loves mixing magic with the Australian bush. Further examples of this are the portal-fantasy *Sanctuary* series about Edge, a 13-year-old girl forced to move to a small country town because of witness protection (the first book is *Where Shadows Rise*) and the forthcoming young adult *Storm Foxes* series about magic and mental health.

Amy has also written the humorous fantasy *Kaditeos* series, following newly graduated Evil Overlord Mercury as she attempts to acquire a castle, and a whole host of non-fiction.

INKLETS

Collect them all! Released on the 1st and 15th of each month.

INKLET #031
Welcome to Dark Dale
LIANA BROOKS

INKLET #032
When War Came to Town
A Powers Story
AMY LAURENS

INKLET #033
Not Fantasy
AMY LAURENS

INKLET #034
Courting the Winter Prince
LIANA BROOKS

INKLET #035
At the Home of the Winter King
A Storm Powers Story
AMY LAURENS

INKLET #036
With This Ring
AMY LAURENS

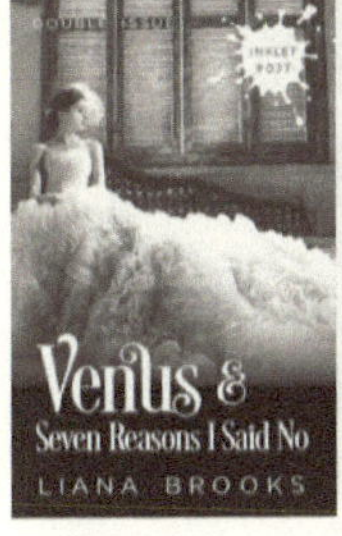
INKLET #037
Venus &
Seven Reasons I Said No
LIANA BROOKS

INKLET #038
OATH KEEPER
AMY LAURENS

INKLET #039
FORGET
A Powers Story
AMY LAURENS

INKLET #040
NOT QUITE
Cinderella
LIANA BROOKS

INKLET #041
ONE BAD MAN
AMY LAURENS

DOUBLE ISSUE
INKLET #042
The Claustrophobia
Of Loneliness &
Adam, Be A Star
AMY LAURENS

INKLET #043
The Artist
as a Young Girl
LIANA BROOKS

INKLET #044
CONFESSIONS
AMY LAURENS

INKLET #045
But For Snow
A Kaitos Story
AMY LAURENS

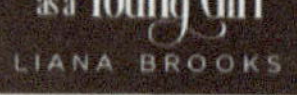

INKLET #046
The Boy
Named NO
LIANA BROOKS

INKLET #047
Anamata
AMY LAURENS

INKLET #048
A Wolf For
Christmas
AMY LAURENS

www.ingramcontent.com/pod-product-compliance
Lightning Source LLC
Chambersburg PA
CBHW051301190726
48286CB00004B/1213